I0639500

Janet Logie Robertson

New Songs of Innocence

Janet Logie Robertson

New Songs of Innocence

ISBN/EAN: 9783337007768

Printed in Europe, USA, Canada, Australia, Japan

Cover: Foto ©Andreas Hilbeck / pixelio.de

More available books at **www.hansebooks.com**

NEW

SONGS OF INNOCENCE

BY

JANET LOGIE ROBERTSON

EDINBURGH

MACNIVEN AND WALLACE

LONDON : DAVID STOTT, 370 OXFORD ST.

1889

CONTENTS

IN pure white novice-garments drest,
    She sleeps, my fairest one,
  Hands folded on her baby breast—
    A little praying nun.
Calm in her innocence she lies,
    At peace with earth and heaven,
With neither woes to make her wise
    Nor sins to be forgiven.

On guard beside my sleeping bliss,
    I see as in a dream
The light of innocence like this
    In countless chambers gleam.
I watch by many a happy hearth
    The joys that children bring,
They put a girdle round the earth
    Of everlasting Spring!

O cherish children, high and low,
    And love them, low and high!
New souls, within our care to grow,
    The hostage of the sky—
Young angels, though their wings be furled,
    The hope that heaven lends
To cast a halo o'er the world
    Their purity defends!

A LULLABY.

LITTLE feet that fain would run,
   Hands that move in unison,
   Eager eyes of ocean blue
Seeking something yet to do—
   Ah, my baby, lie and rest
   Longer on a loving breast !

O that through a meadow sweet
Still might fare these little feet !
That these hands, so seldom still,
Might escape the touch of ill !
   Ah, my baby, lie and rest ;
   Life is good, but love is best.

TRUTH IN LOVE.

JEWEL in my bosom set,
 Tell me, do you love me yet?
 Am I great and good and wise
In my little baby's eyes?
I, who in my soul am nought
But a wavering mist of thought,
Might with sunlit glory shine,
If you loved me, baby mine.

But when you are older grown,
Shall I lose your love, my own?
Will you look upon me then
From the outer world of men?
Will you blame me when you see
Words and actions disagree?
Let the world think as it will—
O my baby, trust me still!

Ere the earthy vapours rise,
To bedim these clear blue eyes,
Look on me, for I am true,
Worthy in my love of you.
When this cloud of life is past,
And the open heaven at last
Welcomes all the race of men,
You will see my truth again.

THE MOON PRINCE.

YESTER eve my prince and I
From our window watched the sky;
Through the branches bare and brown
Of our elm, the moon looked down—
Looked inquiring at my prince!
I've been troubled ever since.

Often had I wondered where
Got my prince that regal air,
And that smile so fair and full,
As of one that's born to rule—
Now I know, alas! too soon;
He's a scion of the moon!

Heedfully at eve must I
Hide my treasure from the sky;
Curtains drawn and lamps alight
May defy the searching night;
While the lone moon waits without
Longing for my prince, no doubt!

THE MOORLAND.

THE long low marshy moorland, with its
    rushes and its reeds,
  Its stunted saughs and willows, its
    melancholy weeds,
The black ooze creeping snakelike under all its
  green—oh why
Need such a dreary place as this have met my
  Willie's eye?

The silver Earn twines lovingly about its fertile
  strath;
A fairy birchwood beckons us along our onward
  path;
And yonder into heaven, a hill's soft rounded
  bosom swells—
Let's leave this lone forsaken moor, and go where
  beauty dwells.

The golden sky looks graciously upon the gentle
  hills
And joyous streams, and with its smile the whole
  green valley fills;
It looks upon the moorland too with just as loving
  eye—
Why should not Willie smile upon what's smiled
  on by the sky?

THE VOICE OF EVENING.

ILLIE and I were resting
    Close by the side of a wood,
    Just when the birds were nesting
Safe in its solitude.
' Coo,' said the cushat, dreaming ;
    ' Love is so sweet ; coo, coo ! '
Willie's blue eyes were beaming,
    And my heart said it too.

The sun went down before us
    In a steady blaze of gold ;
And, one wide billow, o'er us
    The sky's blue ocean rolled.
Behind us the moon came peeping
    Shyly over the trees—
' Is he gone ? is the world all sleeping ?
    May I venture across the seas ? '

' Coo ! ' said my Willie sweetly ;
    ' Coo ! ' said the dreaming dove.
Come, little moon, completely ;
    Nothing 's awake but Love !
Love in the forest dreaming,
    Love in the blue unfurled,
With light beyond it, beaming
    Love on a weary world !

BACK IN TOWN.

WILLIE and I together
    Frolic the livelong day ;
    Be 't sunny or cloudy weather,
  Our business is to play !
In the country the green leaves rustle,
  And the blue sky clasps it all ;
In the town there 's noise and bustle,
  And the houses close like a wall.

But in town we have the people,
  And the different ways of life ;
And our friend the tall church-steeple
  With his weathercock of a wife.
He stands so stiff and steady ;
  She flutters about in the sun,
And dreams she 's a bird already—
  Poor painted image of one !

We smile to the patient horses,
  And the dogs that scamper past,
Till we 're left to our own resources
  When the daylight fades at last.
Then one other comes in beside us,
  And our hopes no longer roam ;
With happy hearts we hide us
  In our sanctuary of home !

THE WORLD FROM OUR WINDOW.

OUT of the high third story
   My little nestling peeps,
   While past, in its pomp and glory,
The world beneath him sweeps:
Here there's a princess married—
   The fairest, of course, and the best ;
Yonder's a hero carried
   Noisily to his rest.

What they're at present admiring
   I cannot tell at all :
A poem inspired and inspiring,
   Or a noted criminal.
For of all the faculties under
   The sun, they possess in full
The faculty of wonder
   At things not according to rule.

On their coursers so fleet and fiery
   The great go careering by—
We sit in our lofty eyry,
   My heart's own nestling and I.
Of our view they cannot scrimp us ;
   My little one watches the show
And laughs like a god on Olympus
   At the freaks of the world below !

. THE COMMON JOYS.

THIS bleak and black November,
  When light has left the sky,
  It's pleasant to remember
The glories of July.
The summer sun was mellow,
  The summer air was mild
When through the cornfields yellow
  I bore my little child.

A wondering laverock started
  Before us from the grass ;
The golden wheat-ears parted
  Bowing, to let us pass ;
The poppies stared, and rounder
  The gazing oxeyes grew ;
From clover-bloom that bound her
  A wanton wild-bee flew.

Came near and nearer gliding
  In undulating sheen,
Upon the corn-tops riding,
  The wind, that walks unseen.

Her breath of balm about us
  Fell like a mantle's fold,
And care was cast without us,
  And time from off us rolled.

My little king sat singing
  In triumph full and sweet,
While earth and air were bringing
  Their tribute to his feet.
The clouds upon my spirit
  Were melted in his mirth,
So glad did he inherit
  The common joys of earth!

THE COMMON SORROWS.

OUT of the pleasant meadows,
    Ablaze with noonday light,
    Into the vale of shadows,
  Into the gathering night,
With trembling feet I wander,
  And fears unowned and wild,
To some dark goal out yonder,
  Bearing my little child.

So gaily he is singing,
  Secure upon my arm,
Close to my bosom clinging,
  Without a dream of harm ;
And I, my heart near breaking,
  Must answer gaily too,
Striving with eyes dull aching
  To pierce the darkness through.

It may be heaven is hidden
  Behind these vulture-wings,
That droop at once, unbidden,
  O'er fairest earthly things.
So useless sight and eyes are
  Against their silent pall,
My darling here is wiser,
  That will not look at all !

A BIRTHDAY.

WHEN you were born, my Willie,
   The wild March winds were out ;
Though their breath was somewhat chilly,
   They gave you a hearty shout.
They told you not to weary,
   For Summer was on her way—
There 's a winter long and dreary
   For the baby that 's born to-day !

Poor little pale-faced stranger,
   With the appealing eyes,
Into a world of danger
   Dropped by the heedless skies !
Yes, you will live your lifetime
   To its appointed close ;
But a peace-time, or a strife-time ?
   That 's what nobody knows.

' A happy New Year ! ' they 're saying
   In the cold grey morning street ;
In the churches, too, they 're praying
   Fair paths for the young year's feet.
Well, life is much as you take it,
   A trial or a triumph, say I ;
The year will be glad if you make it—
   And Willie is going to try !

THE SPRING.

WHILE clouds dissolve in vain regrets
    Around the wintry morn,
    I feel the scent of violets —
And straight the Spring is born !
Again from out a fragrant wood
    Of larches, dropping green,
The wind of March, in merry mood,
    Comes blowing fresh and clean.

Not yet the Spring alights on earth —
    She hovers in the air ;
The budding boughs, the breezes' mirth
    Proclaim her presence there.
The birds are caught in glad surprise,
    And all begin to sing—
My Willie looks with wondering eyes ;
    He cannot see the Spring.

My Willie looks with wondering eyes
    Of bravest, brightest blue ;
Not clearer are those cloudless skies
    The wind of March sweeps through.
The Spring is coming, did I say ?
    Why, 'tis already here !
We 've had Spring with us every day
    In Willie, all the year.

SCARECROWS.

DO you hear his old bones rattling
    And the knocking of his knees?
    It 's not very easy battling
With such a boisterous breeze.
His rags have their mockery heightened
    By a far too respectable hat—
Surely my Willie 's not frightened
    At such a scarecrow as that?

Not he; he 's not so silly;
    He thinks it a capital joke—
Have you any courage, my Willie,
    To spare for us older folk?
For we, who are so much bigger
    And stronger and wiser than you,
Might cut a ridiculous figure
    If our cowardice you knew.

There are scarecrows have dominion
    Over our hearts so small;
There 's one called Public Opinion
    About the worst of them all.
It frowns on us all, man and woman,
    And shakes its wise head of wood
Whene'er we do anything human
    Or try to do anything good.

RENEWAL.

SOME of our hopes were gathered duly;
    Others, we saw, would never be;
    Others again, considered newly,
Lost their desirability.
Life we had gauged—except by sinning—
    Found its pleasures, rewards, and fame
Scarcely worth an immortal's winning—
    Then to the rescue my Willie came.

What did you do? Oh, nothing, nothing—
    What could these little fingers do?
Only revived the gay, green clothing
    Our bare boughs in spring-time knew.
Leaf and blossom, and sweet bird-singing,
    Sheen of sunshine, and scent of May
Still to the bowers of life were clinging,
    As though a curtain had dropped away.

Yes, from our eyes a veil was lifted:
    Life was not meant for us alone;
You were the goal to which we drifted,
    Yours the heritage we would not own.
Often we sighed o'er the vanished treasure
    Left in youth, ere its worth we knew—
Oh, my Willie, it's twice the pleasure
    Living life over again with you!

SAFETY.

PUT your dear little arms round my
    neck, love,
  And lay your soft cheek to mine,
And draw me up safe on deck, love,
  Out of the bitter brine.
Out of the stormy ocean
  That's roaring and raging wild
Round the ark of my devotion
  To my little innocent child.

There's sorrow outside, my Willie !
  There's trouble, and care, and woe ;
And Fortune's smiles are chilly—
  But you are too young to know.
But in here there's peace and pleasure,
  And freedom from earthly harms,
And an inexhaustible treasure—
  In the clasp of these little arms !

The magic circle this is,
  Where nothing ill can come,
The mark that Malice misses,
  Where Slander's voice is dumb.
Ah, hate is weak beside true love,
  As right is stronger than wrong !
I've heaven on my side when I've you, love—
  And may not I well be strong ?

SUNDAY.

THIS is Sunday morning;
  Beneath a smiling sky,
  All in their best adorning,
 The folks go thronging by.
'Vanity!' is the preacher's
 Calvinistic cry;
'We're miserable creatures,
 And only born to die!

Delight on earth's a fiction
 That pious hearts decline;
The water of affliction
 To us must taste divine.'
I wonder if he thinks so
 When he sits down to dine?
I wonder why he drinks so
 His costly earthly wine?

The sky is blue, my Willie,
 The sun shines out o'erhead
As they leave the churchyard chilly,
 Whose breath is of the dead.
And some will look to heaven,
 But some will look to earth,
And spend the holy even
 In mad oblivious mirth.

DETHRONEMENT.

DEAR, they tell you your reign is ended
    With this little new life begun—
    Poor little king, unthroned, unfriended,
  In an eclipse of the sun!
Oh, belovèd, could you believe them?
  How should they know what we think, we two?
It is so easy to deceive them,
    Even our kisses do.

You, my first fair rose of summer,
  Promise and perfect joy in one,
How could a lovelier later comer
    Move me as you have done?
You were my first white star of even;
  Yours the earliest spirit hand
Stretched to me from the hills of heaven,
    Out of the unknown land!

Ah, belovèd, you need not fear me!
  I am not faithless to my first
Watching this new-lit lamp so near me,
    Lent to me to be nursed.
Knit in a closer union rather,
  You and I are to guard its flame
Back to the hands of our heavenly Father,
    Out of Whose heart it came!

LITTLE WILLIE'S PRAYER.

FATHER in heaven! Whose love is more
      Than fondest earthly fathers know;
    Whose shadow walks behind, before,
And guards my youth from every foe;
Whose power has called me from the deeps
    Of life unborn, and given me birth,
And set me in the spring that keeps
    For ever young this lovely earth—

Must I, to whom Thou givest all,
    Thy nursling hanging on Thy breast,
For ever and for ever call
    For greater gifts, and ne'er be blest?
Dost Thou require ev'n thanks from me,
    Thy youngest and Thy feeblest one?
I will look up and smile to Thee
    Like any daisy in the sun!

And shouldst Thou on some coming day,
    In that wise providence of Thine,
See fit to take the light away
    That on my path Thou lettest shine—

I will not speak a fretful word,
    But wait upon Thee then as now,
As patient as a little bird
    Trembling upon a leafless bough.

Father, I cannot pray to Thee!
    I feel Thine arms around me still;
I can but clasp Thee silently,
    And let Thy love my bosom fill.
I cannot think of grief or sin—
    I only know Thou lovest me;
And sings with joy my heart within,
    And soars from earth to dwell with Thee.

THE KNIGHT-ERRANT.

'GOOD-BYE!' says Willie, and sets off
        quick
      Down the long green sloping lawn,
Brave little pilgrim! with grandfather's stick,
   And rosy lips tight drawn.
' Good-bye again!' he stops to call
   From the nearest bush's base—
To him it's a spreading oak-tree tall,
   And beyond it unexplored space.

Sturdily, cheerily on he goes,
   Singing, though out of sight,
Bound to conquer his baby foes
   With all his baby might.
Foes enough there are in the field—
   Loneliness, fear, fatigue
First to my young knight-errant yield
   In all their triple league.

Back he comes again, singing still,
   And lays his head on my knee—
With all his winnings my own little Will,
   And safe to come back to me.

My fair white dove, must I send you out
   Still further into the world,
To smirch with sorrow, and sin, and doubt,
   These wings so safely furled ?

Yes, go, my bird ; go forth and fly
   When your wings are fully grown ;
Be yours the freedom of the sky,
   The strength to soar alone.
Nor earthly ill, nor pain, nor smart
   Can sully that fair broad brow,
So long as you keep the innocent heart
   That sings within you now.

WEATHERCOCKS.

WHAT can it be up yonder
    That twinkles and shines in the sun?
  A golden star of wonder,
  Before daylight is done?
So brightly now it 's blazing,
  The sun it seems to mock!
My Willie can't help gazing—
  But it 's only the weathercock.

Round about he dances
  With all the winds that blow,
Enjoying the envious glances
  Of the living birds below;
But a foot held fast in a fetter,
  Though gold may be all the rest—
Ah, little brown birds, far better
  Are freedom of flight, and a nest!

But he 's so high uplifted,
  Thinks Willie, he must be wise;
Not every one is gifted
  To look into the skies.

Though he saw the heaven's formation
  He would neither know nor care ;
It's not the height of the station,
  But the head and the heart that are there.

My Willie, you 'll find surprises
  In this world are the rule :
The man that to fortune rises
  Is sometimes a lucky fool ;
A prince is often a peasant,
  Whose deeds his dress bemock ;
And many a priest at present
  Is only a weathercock.

AT THE LOCH-SIDE.

THE willows wade in the water
　　Down at the dark loch-side;
　To the boatman's little daughter
They are trusty friends and tried.
Of her it is they 're dreaming
　The long, lone winter through;
For her in spring they 're teeming
　With silver catkins new.

My Willie here has wandered
　The sunny uplands o'er,
Where every season squandered
　. The riches of her store.
For him the spring brought gowans,
　The summer roses shed,
And autumn's ruddy rowans
　Still cluster o'er his head.

He looks at the deep dark water,
　And the dismal willows now :—
The boatman's little daughter,
　She knows them, leaf and bough.
All her life she has played there,
　And missed nor joy nor grace—
But Willie stands dismayed there
　At the sorrow of the place!

THE WINTER SANCTUARY.

THIS dark and dreary winter eve,
   When earth is bare and brown,
   And homeless winds despairing grieve,
  And the cold stars look down—
Come, look into the fire, my dear,
  The ruddy glowing fire!
There's summer warmth and radiance here
  When summer suns retire.

See what a fairy world of bloom,
  Of living bloom and light,
Is prisoned in our little room
  This dreary winter night!
A garden lit with golden flame,
  A grove where sunset glow
Still lingers lovingly—the same
  We watched so long ago!

It is the only radiance
  The cheerless winter knows—
A little corner of romance
  Within a world of prose.
And loving hearts and careful hands
  Must tend the holy fire—
The sanctuary that waiting stands,
  That wandering souls desire.

THE PORTRAITS.

PROPERLY placed and labelled,
　　Each portrait looks from its frame,
　　With his character, real or fabled,
　Affixed to the dead man's name :
This one was good, and was martyred ;
　That one was bad, and a king !
Yon one his soul's peace bartered
　For some poor pitiful thing.

Pilloried they stand there ;
　The gallery 's ever full ;
There 's always a noisy band there
　Of children going to school.
They point with scornful fingers
　When one marked ' Wicked ' they see,
And his crime in their memory lingers,
　With the thought, ' How much better are we ! '

They hang there to all generations,
　Despised and reviled by all,
Forgotten their strong temptations,
　Only remembered their fall.

And maybe an enemy drew them,
   And sent them down to us
With a skewer of spite stuck through them,
   Labelled and libelled thus!

Is this a meaningless mystery,
   My Willie? But it's true.
The gallery of history
   Will open soon to you.
Nowadays Fashion's a fetter
   That keeps us from many a fall;
Remember, though we know better,
   The dead know best of all!

DREAMLAND IN WINTER.

JUMP in, my Willie, and draw up tight
    The cover of eider-down ;
     It 's many a mile we 'll go to-night
Away from the sleeping town.
All day our carriage waiting stands,
    Immovable it seems ;
But now, take the reins in your own little hands—
    We 're off to the land of dreams !

It 's a frosty night, and the stars hang low,
    Like lamps let down from heaven ;
And hard as iron inlaid with snow
    Is the road o'er which we 're driven.
And further still, and further north,
    With the flight of a wild-bird's wing,
Till the hills from their winter hoods look forth
    To hear what news we bring.

On, past these solemn Pharisees,
    The pines, in all their pride,
Scowling upon the leafless trees
    That shiver by their side :

The birch, with penitential air,
  In loveliness of woe ;
The oak, that stood as stately there
  Long centuries ago.

On, on, and ever on we glide
  Upon our glassy way ;
The hopes that night and winter hide
  To us are clear as day.
Till lo, from out the eastern sky
  The light of dawning gleams !
Our steeds break loose, and frightened fly —
  We drop from the land of dreams.

THE WHITE PEACE.

TURRET and battlemented wall
    Are picked out white with snow,
    And roofs of slate, and tiles, and all
The straggling sheds below.
On all alike it lies, and stills
    Their motley discord down ;
One wide white peace harmonious fills
    The temple of the town.

As noiseless o'er the muffled street
    The hurrying figures go,
The chariots with their coursers fleet,
    The wagons creeping slow,
Wild fancies in their elfin hosts
    My brain begins to hive—
This is a city, sure, of ghosts,
    And we alone alive !

Are we alive ?   For answer slips
    A nestling hand in mine,
And bravely in the stars' eclipse
    My Willie's blue eyes shine.
Earth may dissolve beneath our feet,
    And heaven be hid above,
But there 's a refuge safe and sweet
    In living human love !

CHRISTMAS MORNING.

THE crimson of Christmas morning
    Emblazons the cold grey sky,—
A scroll that has met but scorning
From all the years gone by.
'To God in the highest, glory !
    On earth peace ; goodwill to men ! '
But the writing is red and gory—
    A sword has been the pen.

Down all the long dark ages
    That prophecy has come ;
And still the world's fight rages
    As though to drown thee dumb,
O pitiful Voice ! that criest,
    Still vainly, but ever again,
' Glory to God in the highest ;
    On earth peace ; goodwill to men ! '

Deaf are the proud oppressors
    And the spiritless oppressed ;
Defiant the bold transgressors,
    Indifferent the rest.

C

The world has grown old and hoary
    In struggles that never cease ;
And who gives God any glory,
    And where upon earth is peace ?

Willie, my heart's own angel,
    Is there ought that we can do
To spread that old evangel
    And bring its promise true ?
Be ours, O Spirit that sighest
    Through the storm-rifts, now and again,
' Glory to God in the highest ;
    On earth peace ; goodwill to men ! '

IN THE DARKNESS.

OVER the mountains and over the lakes
    Wanders the little lonely moon;
    Nothing else in the darkness wakes—
Even her light will leave us soon.
Over the hills it drops—'tis gone!
The billows of night roll on, roll on.

Silence sits here among the hills;
    Only the voice of the waterfall
All the ear of the darkness fills
    With a ceaseless sighing call,
In its monotony sublime—
Listen, my child, 'tis the voice of Time!

Through the darkness and through the day
    Time runs on, and our lives are done:
Little lives, be they glad or grey;
    Little this world's good, lost or won.
Use well the moments as they flee,
But wait, my child, for eternity!

THE LITTLE PILGRIM.

OVER against our cottage home
 Rises calm a mountain-dome,
  On whose green and rounded crest
Arks of cloud will often rest.
Bare, it is an altar solely;
Veiled, a sanctuary holy;
And when morning mists arise—
Lo, the smoke of sacrifice!

Willie, my poet three years old,
Saw the sun set there in gold;
Long he looked, his large blue eyes
Catching the glow of Paradise.
'Mother,' he said, 'I say in my prayer,
Our Father in heaven—now heaven is there!
Give me my staff; ere the gold grows dim
I will go up the hill to Him!'

Dear little pilgrim, staff in hand,
Journey we all to the promised land!
Many a valley, many a hill,
Lengthen our way with good and ill.
O may He who sits above
Prosper our journey with His love,
Drawing us through the infinite vast
Safely into His arms at last!

MOTHER AND CHILD.

NTO the forest dark and wild
Peers with timorous glance a child,
Ignorant what horror sleeps
In the silence of its deeps—
Ignorant, yet fearing all—
Till from the wood a well-known call
Welcomes him, and his terrors fly,
And joyfully sounds his answering cry,
    ' I am coming, mother.'

Long on the edge of the land unknown
Lingers a soul, afraid, alone ;
Wistfully questions the silent gloom
That curtains from earth the inner room ;
Till from the darkness a voice is heard,
Faint as the note of a far-off bird,
And the old love reaches the soul that waits,
And he answers, drawn through the silent gates,
    ' I am coming, mother ! '

WAITING.

DEAR little bed, so soft and white,
    That waits my wandering Will to-
        night—
Most like an open lily-cup
To fold a weary elfin up—
Thy sheets of innocence be spread,
And peace the pillow for his head,
And dovelike dreams of gentle joy
Hover around my sleeping boy !

If haply in the years to come
No waiting love may light him home,
If no fond mother's hand may spread
The pillow of his lonely bed,
Yet may the white-winged hovering train,
The doves of innocence, remain—
A halo in the darkest night
Circling his soul with heaven's own light !

MORNING ON THE HILLS.

THE wet wheel-tracks are shining
　　Like serpents in the sun,
　　As, twisting and entwining,
　Up the steep hill-road they run.
It 's a long road, my Willie,
　And rough for these little feet;
But if the way is hilly,
　The morning air is sweet.

Look back!　The mists are lifting
　From the sleeping world below;
Between it and us they 're drifting
　On the mountain-side, like snow.
It glitters in new adorning,
　The fair green world so wild!
It smiles to heaven in the morning
　As glad as a waking child.

But what are yon shining lances
　That pierce the peaceful sky,
Hard and sharp as the glances
　Of an unloving eye?

The spires of a siren city
    That lures men with a spell,
That one day, more 's the pity,
    May lure my Willie as well.

Up here, on the lonely mountains,
    Life is a simple thing;
There 's truth in the voice of fountains
    And trust in the wild-bird's wing.
Then seek the hills to rest you
    If, manlike, you must roam—
The morning love that blest you,
    The safe green hills of home!

THE BROTHERS.

THE pines, like a Roman legion,
    March up the mountain side
    To the bleak and barren region
Where the drooping birks abide.
Each birk is a gleaming fountain
    Of unavailing tears;
The pines will carry the mountain,
    Like the Romans in bygone years.

Don't look so sad, my Willie;
    Though Poesy be driven
From her perch on earth most hilly,
    She has all the scope of heaven.
She has wings that well can bear her
    O'er the mounting flood of Prose;
In our ark, too, we could spare her
    A chamber, if she chose.

Why are your eyes so troubled?
    Here comes your joy and mine,
Who all our joy has doubled—
    As straight as a mountain pine.
Like a conqueror he advances;
    Like a drooping birk are you—
There will never be hostile glances,
    I hope, between you two.

My Celt, with the grace of motion
　　In your supple limbs that lies;
With the passion and pain of ocean
　　In the depths of your great grey eyes;
And you, little sturdy Roman,
　　Or Saxon, or what you will,
With your front to friend or foeman,
　　And your mind unchanging still—

Which will better face the dangers
　　Of the pilgrimage of life?
The thrusts of unmeaning strangers,
　　The throes of inward strife?
I ask not which will achieve most
　　Of what men call success;
In happiness I believe most,
　　And a love that grows not less.

My sons, could I unravel
　　The skein of Time for you—
How far these feet must travel,
　　How much these hands must do—
I might weep for the pain and sorrow
　　My little ones must endure;
But I look to a kinder morrow
　　The wounds of earth to cure!

OVERDUE.

WHEN November leaves are whirling o'er
the lea,
    Wild November winds are rifling every
tree,
While I wait and watch beside a stormy sea
For a little ship that is coming home to me.

All the summer through have I waited idly here;
Winds were soft and wooing, skies were calm and
clear;
Like a sheet of crystal shone the water-way—
But her snowy sail never dipped into the bay.

O my little ship, did you linger in the West,
Far among the radiant cloudy islands of the blest,
Breathing airs of heaven, and gathering blossoms
blown
From the trees of Paradise to bear to lands unknown?

Hear me, angry ocean! Hear me, sullen sky!
Hear, and let my little ship all unscathed go by—
Not the topmost pennant of her sail be tempest-
tossed,
Not the frailest fragment of her wondrous cargo lost!

O my little ship, with your precious foreign freight,
Welcome to your haven, howsoever late !
Come, as comes a sunbeam darkest days to cheer—
Come and make a summer in the winter of the
   year !

IN OUR NEST.

LOW in our nest my bird and I
Cower together, and watch the sky;
Many a cloud on pinions fair
Hovers and floats through the higher air ;
Many a bird from earth upsprings
Rapt in the wild free joy of wings—
Low in our nest my bird and I
Look and let them all go by.

Now from their summer nests are driven
Ruthlessly all the winds of heaven ;
Whispering low or blustering loud
Past they go, the noisy crowd :
Sorrow for summer, hope of spring—
That is the sum of their murmuring—
Low in our nest my bird and I
Listen and let the winds go by.

Low in the lap of a favoured vale,
Nor winter's hate nor winter's hail
Reaches our nest so soft and warm,
Where sleeps my baby on my arm.
Still untouched by the skirt of Time
Are the blossoms of love that o'er it climb—
Low in our nest my bird and I
Rest and let the world go by !

LITTLE JAMIE.

INTER winds may rage without,
Mist and rain be blown about,
Summer surely put to flight—
Yet he lingers here to-night!
For my chamber blooms and glows
With the red flame of a rose,
Fresh, and fragrant, and as fair
As the summer roses were.

Yes! my chamber thrills with joy,
Laughing in a rosy boy,
In whose blood the gathered glee
Mantles, of his summers three.
Full of lusty life and mirth,
And the wholesome love of earth,
He defies the influence drear
Wafted from the fading year.

Willie, with his moonlit gaze
Far removed from mortal ways,
Looks down curiously upon
This mirth-filled phenomenon—

From his eyes the mystic ray
Fades to common light-of-day,
And our cloud-rapt vagrant wild
Drops, a happy human child.

Little Jamie! with the eyes
Clear and full as summer skies;
And the warm and winning air,
Frank as sunshine; and the hair
White as hayricks were in June;
And the happy heart in tune
With all nature's harmony—
You are summer's self to me!

MY JOY.

Y maiden with the mystic eyes
　　That caught their colour from the skies,
　　And look on earth without surprise,

How many memories I trace
Of beauty dead and vanished grace
In the sweet oval of thy face!

Upon that smooth pale rounded cheek,
The shadowy Graces of the Greek
A refuge from oblivion seek;

And when a dimple wakens there,
Like sunshine in a garden fair,
They wake, and wear a warmer air.

And thou art then a Joy of eld!
Such as the happier world beheld
Ere joy was quenched and youth was quelled.

A marble Grecian Joy art thou,
Restored to life, and living now,
And smiling with unaltered brow.

And dost thou marvel at our mood
Who deem no beauty born of good
Without the test of pain withstood?

Our Beauty looks through tear-dimmed eyes
From sodden earth to cloudy skies—
She is too sorrowfully wise!

But nought of sorrow dost thou know;
Thou smil'st on earth and all its woe,
And I would have thee ever so.

We worship at the shrine of Pain;
Our glorious robes with grief we stain,
And fret to make them clean again.

We choose the thorns and leave the flowers;
Despising Eden's fragrant bowers,
We claim the desert soil for ours.

But thou art fresh from Eden's land,
Fresh from thy Maker's forming hand,
With hopes we may not understand.

Unfettered yet by human law,
Unvexed by pity, fear, or awe,
But formed complete without a flaw,

D

And filled with joy's delicious wine,
Straight from the source of life divine,
The holiness of health is thine!

Could we but keep them pure and whole,
The body fair, the stainless soul,
Beneath our pitiful control!

We cannot?   Then the fault be ours,
The thorns, the sad regretful showers;
Be thine God's sunshine and His flowers!

THE PARTING YEAR.

NOTHER year is leaving earth
    The richer for its pains :
Of myriad buds that owed it birth
    But little trace remains,
Yet in our garden blooms secure
    Above the circling snows
A newborn flow'ret white and pure—
    A little winter rose !

Two other blossoms grace our tree—
    The first, a hope of Spring ;
The second, Summer's full and free
    And radiant offering.
But Spring and Summer both were fled,
    And Autumn winds blew wild,
When this sweet bud upreared its head—
    A gentle woman-child !

My daughter !   As upon my knee
    In smiling trust she lies,
Without one fear of ills to be
    To cloud her clear blue eyes,

My own uncouth forebodings flee
   Before that winsome face ;
For even earth, to such as she,
   May prove a pleasant place !

O little woman ! may you grow
   As wise as you are fair ;
And what you meet of woman's woe
   May you have strength to bear !
But wear not weeds of woe by choice,
   Nor swell the common moan ;
Rather in others' joy rejoice,
   And cheer them with your own.

Envy no man his work, nor ask
   To rule by sword or pen ;
We women have a nobler task —
   The moulding of the men !
And still remember that *to be*
   Is better than *to do* —
Thus more may bless, as well as we,
   The year that gave us you !

THE BIRDS.

ITHOUT, the snow is whit'ning
　　All patient earthly things—
　　When, swift as summer lightning,
There's a flash of fluttering wings,
And a soft red bosom beating
　　Against the frozen pane,
And two bright eyes entreating
　　For aid, and not in vain.

Swift glance up from my bosom
　　Two other eyes of blue—
Two flower-like eyes, that blossom
　　The barren winter through.
And they too are appealing
　　For entrance and for aid,
In this new country feeling
　　Alone yet and afraid.

O trembling bird without there,
　　O bird upon my breast,
The love ye ask and doubt there
　　Can never be expressed :

My love so fain would cover
　　All helpless earthly things
With the passion of a lover,
　　With a mother's patient wings !

But the love I scarce can utter
　　In a finite heart is furled :
Birds are we all, and flutter
　　On the brink of another world.
At the window of heaven gather
　　Tired wings and wistful eyes —
Open it wide, O Father,
　　To every bird that flies !

LOVE'S COMPENSATION.

Y lily fair and undefiled,
    My pure and holy maiden-child,
    With eyes by earthly dews unwet,
And mouth serenely smiling yet
At memories of things unseen—
We who have longer banished been
Forget these visions of the skies
And look to earth with blinded eyes.

From fields of never-failing flowers
You come to this cold world of ours :
In this bleak world, so wintry bare,
Our exile you have come to share.
And what have we to offer you
For blossoms of celestial hue
And all the blissful bowers above
You left for us—but only love ?

O life it is a weary toil
In bodies rooted to the soil,
Inspired to soar, but wanting wings,
Choked in a fog of common things !

Each rising joy beat back by rain,
Each budding pleasure nipped by pain—
What is there that this earth can give
To make our life less hard to live?

The pinnacle of power is high,
But is it nearer to the sky?
The richest food at wealth's control
Can never feed a starving soul;
And what is man's desire for fame,
But that his knowledge and his name
May touch with love his fellow-men
And win reward of love again?

Love is the sun, benignly fair,
That warms for us life's chilly air;
Without it, we should fall and freeze
Like mariners on polar seas.
For you, my flower, my lily pale,
May love's pure sunshine never fail, .
But guard you with its holy flame
Back to that heaven from whence you came!

HER FIRST SPRING.

BLACK boughs against a silver sky
    Stand clear, and cold, and bare ;
    Black is the river flowing by,
  And wan the grasses there.
Each torch of beauty blackened lies,
  Bleached every wave of green ;
—And this is all my maiden's eyes
  As yet of earth have seen !

But soon for her shall purple mist
  Enfold each waking tree,
And every field the sun has kissed
  Dimple in daisied glee ;
The river, changed from lead to gold,
  Upon its way shall sing ;
And all the sweets of earth unfold
  For her first earthly spring !

OUR FORTRESS.

WITHIN our castle, maiden mine,
    We dwell secure, and fear no foe;
    Our ramparts are a mountain-line,
A guardian river glides below.
Here from the troublous world apart,
    And raised above its common care,
I dream of heaven with you, my heart,
    And soar from earth in mountain-air.

As o'er our castle wall we lean
    To mark the light of morn or eve
Inform anew the distant scene—
    Ascends the voice of them that grieve.
A wail from out the world's unrest
    Assails our high ethereal calm;
It stirs our peaceful mountain-nest
    That knew no utterance save a psalm.

It lingers ever in mine ear;
    It presses on me when I pray;
The sound of mirth I may not hear
    Till that sad murmur dies away.
For why should we be good and glad
    Within our fortress on the height,
When there are souls ashamed and sad,
    Who cannot rest by day or night?

Nay, from our castle will we go
  With sympathy and succour both,
Down through the sorrowing vales below,
  To aid the meanest nothing loath.
O'er all the world's wide battlefield
  Let all the wounded be our care,
And all the weak who fain would yield
  Our confidence and courage share.

Let no distrust of men be ours,
  Nor any feeble woman's fear ;
Our guidance is a higher Power's,
  Our goal nor gain nor glory here.
More space wherein to live and grow
  The wakened soul within demands ;
But the direction of its flow
  We leave in God our Father's hands.

Still to our fortress of the soul
  At eventide may we retire,
To gain a surer self-control,
  To feed again our secret fire.
Still from our topmost turret high
  Shall wave our banner fair unfurled—
' For truth and right, my girl and I '—
  My girl and I against the world !

MY REFUGE.

FROM vain attempts to show to men
　　The folly of their prejudices,
　　　I turn me to my tower again
That still the lower turmoil misses.
And here I meet my maiden bright—
　　My maiden-moon of spotless splendour—
With eyes of unabated light,
　　And open arms how soft and tender !

O maiden mine, here will we dwell !
　　The world beneath in mist is blended ;
It scoffs at all the dreams we tell,
　　Its hopes are low and narrow-minded.
Here will we sit and spin and weave
　　Our fine-drawn theories and notions,
Nor heed the human waves that heave
　　About our tower in vain commotions.

Here will we sit as lone and far
　　As ladies fair of old enchanted,
Or dwellers in some distant star,
　　Or two new souls in Eden planted.

Forgotten Eden! hidden still
  Behind some forest's green defences,
And holding, to the fearless will,
  Enjoyment both for soul and senses.

But is it hid in space or time,
  This Eden that we seek to enter?
Earth's lofty mountains must we climb,
  Or penetrate her hidden centre?
Or pierce the purpose of the years
  That wait without the Present's portal?
—Or trust in patience till appears
  The gloomy guide to life immortal?

While thus I muse in dull eclipse
  Of that same hope my spirit vaunted,
My maiden lifts her smiling lips
  And questioning eyes of love undaunted.
O darling innocence and truth!
  Flower of my life, my day's bright morrow,
Within the Eden of thy youth
  I rest, and find relief from sorrow.

MY FLOWERS.

Y neighbours set their flowers in pots,
  Their windows' white reserve to
   soften;
Or else in tidy garden plots,—
 And water them, and trim them often.
But mine, though asking all my care,
 And wearing me with vain endeavour
My neighbours' worthy pride to share,
 Are wayward and as wild as ever!

My neighbours' flowers are still and meek;
 They always stay where they are planted.
They never cry—they never speak—
 They could not speak although they wanted!
My flowers no boundary will keep;
 From room to room they run in riot.
Only beneath the power of sleep
 They rest a while in needful quiet.

They watch the sun until he sets,
 They greet him, too, whene'er he rises;
In spite of all my vain regrets
 They fill the house with sweet surprises.
Where will you find a rose as fair
 As Jamie's smiling face, or Willie's?
And my sweet maiden's looks and air
 Are lovelier than a thousand lilies!

THE DYING CHILD.

NOW clover is perfuming
    The meadows every day,
  And every weed is blooming
  Along the dusty way ;
But, all my chamber shading,
  Grief sits beside the bed
Where my sweet flower lies fading
  And cannot raise her head.

The sunshine cannot save her ;
  The breeze's sweetest breath,
The summer's fairest favour—
  They cannot combat Death !
I see the sword hang trembling ;
  I shrink in anguish wild ;
Yet still, my woe dissembling,
  Speak comfort to my child :

' My darling, you are going
  Where I too hope to come ;
Where life's great tree is growing—
  Where sorrow's voice is dumb.
A land of joy and splendour
  Beside a sea of glass,
Lit by a love more tender '—
  —Father, let this cup pass !

THE FISHER.

FROM her home amid the shadows
    Of the quiet mountain-side,
    Down through the sunlit meadows
    She comes, a maiden bride,
Where meadow-sweet and grasses
    All in their white array
Watch for her as she passes,
    And wait upon her way.

' But it is only water ! '
    Says Jamie, looking down
Upon the mountain's daughter
    With a bewildered frown.
One chubby hand holds tightly
    A shining rod and tall,
While strikes the ripple lightly
    His bait—a beech-nut small !

And now he spies a troutlet
    Under the golden wave ;—
His fancy sees no outlet
    That fated fish to save—
When, tranquilly escaping,
    It glides beneath a stone,
And leaves our fisher gaping
    Upon the bank alone !

THE PALADINS.

THE roads we trod in careless strength,
And never thought them long,
Lie now uncoiled to magic length
The devious hills among ;
And softer is their wayside grass,
And dearer are their flowers,
For little feet that fain would pass
In equal pace with ours.

Nor are their end and boundary plain—
For still, to Willie's eye,
Each rising knoll he seeks to gain
Leads straight into the sky !
And still to Jamie's furtive gaze,
That yet the sight would dare,
There lurks in every woody maze
A lion or a bear !

A world of wonders this to both,
Where everything is new,
Where he who stays at home in sloth
No mighty deed may do.
So forth they go like paladins
To make the world their own ;
Who over *self* the battle wins
Will never want a throne !

E

QUEEN O' THE MEADOW.

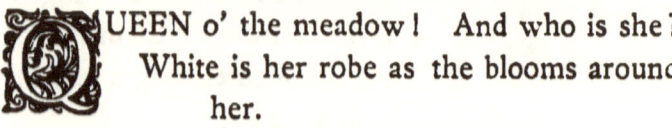

QUEEN o' the meadow !   And who is she ?
 White is her robe as the blooms around
  her.
A gay green sedge shall her sceptre be,
 And with daisy-wreath have her subjects crowned
  her.
Willie shall be her counsellor high—
 His ways are wise, though his words escape her ;
Jamie her admiral—sailing by,
 Observe his fleet, though it 's only paper !

Queen o' the meadow !   She sits and smiles,
 And pulls her daisies all to pieces,
While Will with a book the day beguiles,
 And Jamie a captive bee releases.
Thus through the long bright afternoon
 The queen and her ministers muse together
In golden silence, best in tune
 With the golden calm of August weather.

Queen o' the meadow !   In days to come,
 When your hopes are grown, and your thoughts
  are clearer,
When your lovely lips are no longer dumb,
 And your ways are wiser, though never dearer,

When by alien hearts you are hailed a queen—
  And, it may be, mocked and denied by others—
Will you dream of the days when you reigned
    serene
  In the loyal love of your little brothers?

TO A SLEEPING CHILD.

DEAR little hands that the sun has kissed
    Hanging so helpless now,
    Dear little head with its golden mist
  Veiling the open brow,
Eyelids calm, and lashes curled
    Low on the rounded cheek,
Lips the sweetest in all the world
    If they could only speak.

Under the wave of sleep she lies,
    Warm in its rosy tide;
Pleasures unseen of waking eyes
    Meet her on every side.
See! she smiles with a dreamy grace—
    Ah! little maiden mine,
Dreamland's a lovely dwelling-place
    For innocent souls like thine!

Dear little hands, so helpless now,
    What are they yet to hold?
What are the cares shall line that brow
    Under its mist of gold?
Breathe in her through life's darkest deeps,
    Spirit of purity!
That when at last our darling sleeps,
    Happy her dreams may be.

OUR QUEEN ELIZABETH.

NDERNEATH the orchard-trees
Of a garden full of bees,
Pinks and roses, blossomed beans,
Every fragrant herb that leans
Lowly in its loveliness,
Hiding from the wind's caress,—
Through a cloud of summer breath
Comes our queen, Elizabeth !

Very young and fair is she,
Scarcely reaching to my knee ;
Wise and winsome, good and gay,
Gracious as the summer day.
Dancing to each shadowy stalk
Mirrored on the sunny walk ;
Singing, as the Psalmist saith,
A new song, Elizabeth !

In a garden such as ours,
Filled with fair old-fashioned flowers,
May have roved a baby queen
Sadder far than this, I ween.
Ah, your childhood, good Queen Bess,
Sire-forsaken, motherless !
May no sorrow worse than death
Shadow our Elizabeth !

JACK AND THE BEANSTALK.

JUST down our garden walk, there,
    And halfway to the wall,
    A single stout beanstalk there
Has grown extremely tall.
' It waits for Jack to climb it ;
    And what 's become of him ? '
So said—I only rhyme it—
    Our valiant climber, Jim.

This morning as we wandered
    Adown the garden walk,
While Willie looked and pondered,
    And Jim did all the talk,
Up that same staircase narrow,
    That beanstalk strong and high,
We saw him climb, Jack Sparrow !
    With daring in his eye.

' O Willie, do you see him ?
    With terror he is dumb ;
We 'll keep at hand to free him
    In case the giant come.'
Alas ! not quite reliant
    Are birds on what we say—
Our Jamie was the giant,
    Thought Jack, and flew away !

A CITIZEN OF EARTH.

THROUGH the red sea of grasses
   That trembles and divides,
And falls in fragrant masses
   Before his manful strides,
He comes! with blue eyes beaming
   Beneath his lint-white hair—
The life within them gleaming
   Would light a winter's care.

This is no princely stranger
   From regions fair and far ;
This merry meadow-ranger
   Mourns no deserted star.
These frank and friendly glances,
   The kindness of his mirth,
Proclaim him who advances
   A citizen of earth.

There's pleasure in his coming
   To every living thing,
The bees about him humming,
   The birds upon the wing,

The collie from the farm there
    Exuberant of tail,
The sheep without alarm there
    His welcome advent hail.

At every wayside meeting
    With every ragged child,
He smiles as frank a greeting
    As ever equal smiled;
That some have more than others
    He does not understand;
To all mankind as brothers
    He reaches out his hand.

My Jamie, when the roses
    Have faded from your face,
And manhood's strength deposes
    That fresh and boyish grace,
Hold fast, till to the portals
    Of death those feet have trod,
The brotherhood of mortals,
    The fatherhood of God!

OUR QUEEN MARY.

O Castle Gloom we brought our joys—
Our maiden bright, our gallant boys—
Its rugged steep ascents to dare ;
To breathe its high ethereal air ;
O'er Care and Sorrow both to rise,
Poised midway between earth and skies ;
To light once more with youthful bloom
The Castle and the Hill of Gloom !

O Castle old, of vanished days,
When valour's glow and beauty's blaze
Lit these low halls, so dim and rude,
What memories in thine archways brood !
But most of one long winter's night
When Mary's footfall, fairy light,
Led off the dance that graced beside
The nuptials of a noble bride.

These frowning walls, that erst have seen
The face of Scotland's loveliest queen,
Re-echo now the pattering feet
Of yet another Mary sweet.
For her may in the future wait
A lowlier and a happier fate—
A queen of home, whose crown as fair
Yet wants the weight that monarchs wear.

A DAY OF MIST AT CASTLE GLOOM.

THIS morning, Willie, as we look
  From our accustomed window-
    nook,
Where are the hills and where the glen
That daily welcome us again?
This old grey castle where we dwell
Is surely compassed with a spell,
Wrapt in a cloud, and wildly whirled
About the confines of the world!

No castle this! it is a boat
Loosed from its moorings, and afloat,
Adrift upon a sea of mist:
The winds may bear it where they list.
From this our window-seat we see
No kindly green of grass or tree,
But tossing vapours weirdly white,
Shot through by neither day nor night.

Our cabin here—that was a room—
Is filling fast with filtered gloom,
And clammy fingers, clinging cold,
Our bodies and our spirits hold.

And nearer draws a sound of wail,
And wandering voices faintly hail
Our wandering bark, to set them free
From horrors of that misty sea.

But we will gather round the fire,
Hand linked in hand, a cheerful choir,
And sing of wholesome summer days
On wooded banks and grassy braes.
Thus on our memories will we live
Till sleep a change of prospect give,
And morning find us moored again
Beneath the hills, above the glen!

DOWN THE GLEN.

OME with me, Willie, down the glen
　　Where summer leaves for joy are
　　　shining;
Beyond this frowning castle's ken
　　Are bowers of oak and birk entwining.
The hazel stoops beside the pool,
　　And palm-like rise the feathery ashes,
And under beechen shadow cool
　　The gleam of falling water flashes.

Why, what a strange green world is here
　　Kept hid alike from hill and valley!　·
Beside its streamlets crystal clear
　　The airs of parting summer dally.
Nay, brings not this caressing breeze
　　A breath of life from sources olden?
Survives within this world of trees
　　Ought of the age that men call golden?

I feel a mystic life around
　　In these green labyrinthine mazes;
A voice is hid in every sound,
　　An eye from every covert gazes.

Within that rocky cleft might dwell
  A Naiad yet in peace abiding,
By mossy boulders guarded well,
  In foamy veil her beauties hiding.

What horns are these that next surprise
  Our shelving path above the water?
Crouched in the fern a satyr lies
  In waiting for the river's daughter.
Ah, Willie, let us turn and flee
  Back to our refuge on the mountain!
As little chance for you or me
  As for the Naiad of the fountain!

Here on the height we breathe again
  In calmer, clearer air, though colder.
Farewell the dim secluded glen,
  The dripping rock, the mossy boulder,
The tangled brake that dryads fills—
  'Tis but a place for owls to grope in—
Ours be the freedom of the hill
  That ever unto heaven lies open!

AN AUTUMN EVENING IN KINROSS-SHIRE.

THE sun in regal splendour
    Invests the western sky;
      In light serene and tender
Both hills and valleys lie.
There's peace on earth at even
    When daily toil is done,
And o'er the Vale of Leven
    Streams forth the setting sun.

But yet, my children, hearken!
    As shadows deeper grow
And night begins to darken
    I hear a sound of woe.
Whate'er of peace she borrow,
    Whate'er of waking mirth,
A dread of coming sorrow
    Disturbs the dreaming earth.

In every summer loaning,
    In every leafy tree,
I hear a sound of moaning,
    Like the murmur of a sea;
The wheatfields are repeating
    With spears uplifted high
The gladiator greeting
    Of those about to die!

The wind, that ne'er rejoices,
  Its sympathy has given,
And all these wailing voices
  Salute the silent heaven.
' Alas !' they cry in chorus,
  ' Is there no other way ?
Is there no goal before us
  But darkness and decay ?

' This flame of life that flashes
  In shining blade and leaf —
Has it no end but ashes ?
  No joy to come, but grief?
Is every guileless creature
  That cheers us with its play
A sacrifice to nature—
  To cruel laws a prey ? '

I hear their wail, my children,
  Deep echoed in my heart—
Its dream of love bewildering
  Where everything has part.
The wail of Pagan beauty
  That passes with its breath—
Only the life of duty
  Endures the touch of death

AN ATTEMPTED EVICTION.

FROM this our homely castle,
    Our modest citadel,
        The wind—unruly vassal!—
Would our retreat compel.
He rushes and he rages
    Against our outer wall—
The war with us he wages
    Is useless, after all!

A happy thought comes o'er him,
    And with an awful shout
He drives the rain before him,
    In hopes to drown us out!
But Jamie laughs, and Willie
    Looks on with careless eyes—
No, Wind, we're not so silly;
    Our home you can't surprise!

No, Wind, you'll ne'er be able
    This way to make us quit.
There is an ancient fable—
    Perhaps you've heard of it?
A traveller it spoke of—
    The wind that swept the moors
But couldn't blow his cloak off,
    Was *he* a friend of yours?

THE GARDEN OF THE TOWN.

WE look from our lampless casement
　　Into the lighted street;
　　The wet stones gleam in the base-
　　ment,
　　The cool night air is sweet.
The skies are dewy and tender
　　With stars just out of sight;
There 's a glow of hidden splendour
　　Behind the veil of night.

The lamps we mocked so lately
　　Show now their flowery flames;
The houses tall and stately
　　Stand like patrician dames.
From their dark but shapely masses,
　　Outlined in living fire,
An old enchantment passes,
　　And stirs an old desire.

The dream we dropped comes o'er us,
　　Of pleasure here on earth:
Tired are the wings that bore us
　　From men and social mirth.
Though ours be the upland hilly
　　And the forest-glory brown,
There 's a glamour yet, my Willie,
　　O'er the garden of the town!

A BIRTHDAY GREETING.

RING the bells in every steeple!
Fire the cannons great and small!
Shout with all your hearts, good
people—
Then come listen one and all
Till I tell you what they mean—
'Tis the birthday of a queen!

Ring the bells and fire the cannon!
Cry hurrah! with all your power.
On the banks of Thames or Shannon
Never bloomed a fairer flower
Than this Lady of the North
Born beside the silver Forth!

Yes, this Lady—who may she be?
Scornfully I hear you say.
Well, her foremost title 's *Liebe*,
And her second name is *May*.
Love and Summer we 've within,
Independent of your din!

AN INDIAN IDOL.

ES, Willie, this is an idol
  From a land that the sun is near,
    But where lurid hazes hide all
The heaven we look to here.
Where rice-fields are defended
  By bands of green bamboo;
Where palaces are splendid
  And temples golden too.

There life seems gay and easy,
  In brilliant colours drest,
Unbroken by the breezy
  Impatience of the West.
O'er woods of tangled wonder
  The gaudy blossoms climb—
With monstrous creatures under,
  Asleep among the slime!

By the light of reason's taper
  Their learnèd pundits go,
Where all above is vapour,
  And horror all below.

And those who cannot reason,
　　The untaught poor, down-trod,
What marvel though they seize on
　　A nearer hope than God?

Full many a mother, kneeling
　　At this thing's shrine, has prayed
For heartening or for healing,
　　For comfort or for aid.
And though her cry she uttered,
　　Wild as a helpless bird
Whose nest a snake has fluttered,
　　I think our Father heard!

THE WANING MOON.

I T 'S a cold clear winter morning,
    The sky is frosty blue,
  The round red sun is scorning
The world he looks into.
Like a haughty Turk he rises,
  Aroused from his rest too soon,
And in revelry surprises
  His prisoner, the moon !

Behold her, shrinking pallid
  Before his angry gaze,
Sense nor assurance rallied
  To justify her ways !
And how can she escape there ?
  That sky, so frosty blue,
If it would only gape there
  And let the lady through !

Alas, the helpless lady !
  My boys, what will you dare
For poor Scheherazadé,
  Who greets you, smiling fair,
With pleasant stories nightly ?
  Or must she perish so ?
Perhaps if you ask rightly
  The sun will let her go !

ON THE CANAL.

THE slow canal is surging
　　Like a river tempest-rolled;
　　To-day she needs no urging,
That mare forlorn and old.
Like a kite the gust has caught her—
　The barge glides on behind
Like a wedge driven through the water
　By the hammer of the wind.

Those two old men on board there
　Go daily up and down—
I muse what thoughts are stored there
　Beneath each hoary crown.
What are the joys that brighten
　Their orbit fixed and grey?
Is there a hope to lighten
　Their shortly closing day?

They talk at times together,
　Or smoke the pipe of peace;
Of course there is the weather
　Whose changes hardly cease
To keep them still awake there,
　And cheerful, more or less—
My Willie's heart would break there
　For very weariness!

RAGNARÖK.

ALL night it has blown and blustered;
  And, now it is day once more,
  See you the armies mustered
On heaven's wind-swept shore?
The serried lines are guarded
  By scouts of flying rack;
The sun himself is warded
  By sentinels in black.

.

So wildly the clouds are wedded
  In conflict fiercely dumb,
It seems that the hour long dreaded
  Of Ragnarök is come!
The gods are fighting yonder,
  The evil with the good—
Ah, Willie, watch and ponder—
  Will the evil be withstood?

There's a Ragnarök, my Willie,
  For many a human heart:
The winds of doubt blow chilly,
  The hopes of spring depart.

From Thor the strength is riven,
And Baldur the loved is dead,
And Odin grows old in heaven
And hangs his heavy head.

That hour, in conflict blending
Impartial good and ill,
Fear not! the strife has ending,
In death, or victory still.
Choose you, and hold it strongly,
Your faction in the fight;
Rather than triumph wrongly,
Fall bravely in the right!

THE RIVAL QUEENS.

AIDIE at the window lingers
Looking out into the night
That the moon with fairy fingers
Paints so exquisitely white—
Clearer far than many a grey day—
It is wonderful to Maidie !

Leaf and branch she watches graven
Duly on the dewy sky ;
While within a cloudy haven
Moon and stars at anchor lie.
In this world so cool and shady
She could always dwell, thinks Maidie.

Cheek and brow, the moonbeams greet her ;
In her eyes they find eclipse !
Sweet the young moon's curve—but sweeter
Is the curve of Maidie's lips.
I am anxious and afraid aye
When the moon shines full on Maidie.

Brighter grow the rival glances
   Of the sky's queen and my own ;
Mine to victory advances—
   Be my arms about her thrown
      Lest the moon, the jealous lady,
      Stoop to run away with Maidie !

THE OLD ALBUM.

YES, boys; we 'll open it to-night,—
　　This meeting-house of silent friends
　　In fading finery bedight,—
And talk of them, to make amends
For our unmannerly neglect.
　　Stand one of you on either side;
We 'll stay no longer to reflect,
　　But straight the album open wide.

You smile to see their ancient dress
　　That was so modish in its time;
The ladies' hoops, and helplessness,
　　The men-folk's attitudes sublime.
That boy to be a soldier grew—
　　In the Crimean war he fell;
This other wore a jacket blue,
　　And many a famous yarn could tell.

Ah! now we come to later days;
　　And yet, how different from now
Their looks, their costume, and their ways!
　　To Fashion all indeed must bow.

Here Willie spies a pictured pair
    That takes his fancy for the night :
' Who is the sweet-faced lady there
    Beside the little girl in white ? '

You know the little girl in white ;
    She stays with you, now she is grown.
' Mamma ! ' cries Jamie, in delight ;
    ' The lips and eyes are all your own.'
' But who 's the stranger lady then ? '
    Asks Willie ; ' do we know her ? '   No ;
She died when I was only ten,
    My Willie, many years ago.

' Tell us about her.'   Well, I will —
    The little that I have to tell.
Her grave sweet smile, it haunts me still —
    My father's sister Isabel.
Brief glimpses of her, memory gives ;
    Within the bower that was her room
'Mid faded needlework she lives,
    With music tinkling through the gloom.

She loved an honest man and true,
    And waited for him many a year ;
And when at last their sky was blue
    And all their future golden-clear—

When one short year of wedded life
 Had brought a higher title still
And crowned a mother in the wife—
 She died, by God's most holy will.

She died—and left her baby-boy,
 And left the lover of her youth ;
So short a dream of earthly joy,
 Such strangely-ordered life, in sooth,
Was hers ! Ah, Willie, close the book ;
 God's ways we will not wonder o'er ;
She 'll meet us with that grave sweet look,
 And tell us all, on yonder shore !

OUR CHAMPION.

THE mist drops from his shoulders
　　Down on the kneeling lands,
　　And, clear to all beholders,
A snow-clad giant stands.
Upon his armour hoary
　　The wintry sunbeams glance
With the glamour and the glory
　　Of chivalrous romance.

Well, Willie, do you know him?
　　So cold and strangely gleam
Those winter rays, they show him
　　Like the mountain of a dream.
How many a summer morning
　　We watched for him in vain,
The moody giant—scorning
　　The people of the plain!

His robe of peace was green then,
　　His crest the soft winds kissed,
But, careless to be seen then,
　　He cloaked himself in mist.
And now, when blows defiant
　　The ice-blast of the North,
The stern, stout-hearted giant
　　To succour us comes forth!

AT THE WORLD'S PLAY.

FROM marking the times and the
    seasons
    In our watch-tower next the sky—
The rains, and their cloudy reasons,
    The winds that weirdless fly,
The years that bloom and are buried,
    And yet return again,
Till our hopes o'er Styx are ferried—
    We turn to the world of men.

We look from our box, my children,
    On the ever-busy stage—
Its footlights false, bewildering,
    Its precepts smooth and sage.
So snugly and easily uttered
    By the actors, one and all--
Never a breast seems fluttered
    Save at the prompter's call.

Fashion, the prompter, sits there
    In semblance of a queen ;
She robes unruly wits there
    In garbs uncouth and mean.

But they that ape her gestures,
  And watch her every way,
She gives them lordly vestures,
  And pleasant parts to play.

What is the play? you ask me—
  I'm sure I cannot tell!
To give its plot would task me
  And weary you as well.
Intrigues without an ending
  And never a point at all—
The moral needs amending
  Before the curtain fall!

But Willie, I see you watching
  The stage with eager eyes—
That its liveliness is catching
  There's nobody denies.
The changes and the chances
  Of the uncertain strife;
The mist o'er death that dances,
  That worldly men call life!

You would never be happy yonder
  Amid yon idle crowd.
They rush to the latest wonder
  With joy not deep, but loud,
Like dogs to a bone that's flung them—
  But I need not speak, I see
You would rather be down among them
  Than up in the clouds with me!

THE MOONLIT WORLD.

THERE are six trees against the wall—
    Three true, and three of shadow;
    The moonlight throws our gables tall
Again upon the meadow.
A strange, cool world we dwell in here,
    Removed from daily trouble,
Where all above is sapphire clear,
    And all below is double!

Yes, here with pleasure could we stay,
    In beauty thus benighted,
Although the glaring lamp of day
    Should never more be lighted.
What say you, boys? shall it be done?
    Shall we all night be waking,
And go to sleep whene'er the sun
    Comes o'er our borders breaking?

'We will!' says Willie, kindling bold,
    With moonlit fancies dawning;
But Jamie says, 'It would be cold!'
    And scarce can keep from yawning.
Be off then, both of you, to bed,
    Like kind and loving brothers—
The moon may haunt one's dreaming head,
    The sun still hold the other's!

G

AT THE PANTOMIME.

OUR Jamie with his round blue eyes
  And earnest wondering look,
  Whose life is one serene surprise,
Unwittingly we took,
By way of treat one Christmas-time,
To see a merry Pantomime.

He saw the clown—the clever thief—
  Go stealing with applause ;
He saw the honest come to grief
  By pantomimic laws.
He quite enjoyed the curious clime
And manners of the Pantomime.

And since we brought him home again
  He cannot yet believe
It 's different in the world of men
  From that gay Christmas eve ;
He thinks it 's always Christmas-time,
And all the world 's a Pantomime !

A WINTER SUNRISE.

SPEED on, ye light-winged carriers
    Of hope and heartening new !
    Throw down the night's black
  barriers
And let Apollo through !
Apollo waits without there,
    Curbing his steeds of flame ;
The stars of morning shout there
    The mighty sun-god's name.

He waits, his radiant tresses
    Athwart the blackness blown ;
Against the gates he presses
    That guard Night's ancient throne.
The ebon gates are burning !
    His chariot rushes through,
The throne of Night o'erturning,
    And fires the heavens anew.

' Ye children, sing Apollo ! '
    Ye boys with golden hair,
On earth his footsteps follow,
    And make a sunshine there.

Be yours a summer glory
　　Of glad and hopeful smiles,
To warm the winter hoary
　　Of these cold northern isles !

A WINTER MOONRISE.

THE dream of day is ageing ;
　　His faded flag is furled ;
　　In terror cold and caging
Night stoops upon the world.
The world in darkness waking,
　　It trembles, praying low ;
When, through the blackness breaking,
　　Shines forth Diana's bow !

Behind its light the heaven
　　Regains its heavenly blue ;
The mists afar are driven ;
　　The stars come peeping through.
The mighty maid they greet now,
　　And follow in her train
To chase the clouds they meet now
　　Across the shining plain.

Ye maidens, sing Diana !
　　Queen of the silver bow —
Of whose divine arcana
　　Your lot is cast to know.
Rise on earth's hour of sorrow
　　In pure and lovely light,
Till seems the wished-for morrow
　　Scarce so serenely white !

SCOTTISH SONG.

WILLIE, when your voice I hear
So high and sweet, so true and clear,
The wildly varied notes prolong
Of some neglected Scottish song,
My heart responsive swells, and fills
With memories of heather hills,
And lonely glens, and winds that wail
Down through the years their wordless tale.

And clearer yet the vision grows—
I see the feuds of ancient foes ;
In ' clouds o' reek ' that reach the skies,
The bonnie House o' Airlie lies.
Then, melting to a minor key,
The wandering Prince's woes I see,
As ' sweet and clearly' as of yore
The wee bird sings at my ha' door.

Shall these, our children's heritage,
Be yet denied our children's age ?
In Memory's museum classed
As relics of a barbarous Past ?
Nay, let us at their vocal shrine
Our hearts in human touch combine,
And glad our sordid cares forget
To feel their pity potent yet !

AT MIDNIGHT.

IN the darkness as I lie
    Dreaming, with my children by,
    Watchful even in my dreams
As a mother's care beseems,
Comes a wailing wild and sore,
Pleading at my chamber-door;
Opening in haste, I find
No one but the homeless wind!

As I lay me on my bed,
Free again from drowsy dread,
Comes a knocking on the pane—
No one but the restless rain!
What would wind and rain with me
That they cannot let me be
In my chamber warm and still
That sweet children's breathings fill?

' Sister, leave thy house of clay;   .
Come with wind and rain away.
Taste the freedom of a soul
Glad released from earth's control.'
Nay, my brothers; patience yet!
Think not I your claims forget;
Meanwhile, be your fears dispelled —
I 'm in *happy* bondage held!

IN THE MOONLIGHT.

INTO the moonlight as we gaze—
     That silvers all the miry ways;
     That makes our neighbours' chim-
neys brown
The towers of an Italian town,
And round the naked branches weaves
A glory brighter than of leaves—
My maiden quits my clasp outright,
And stands alone there in the night.

So beautiful, so strange she seems,
Most like a creature of my dreams,
With parted lips and shining eyes
Uplifted to the lustrous skies—
No maid of mortal mould is she,
But some fair spirit, roaming free
From miry earth to mystic heaven,
Of matter by the moonlight shriven !

O maiden, in the moonlight there,
Of face and form unearthly fair,
Back to our empty home return—
Back to the hearts that mortal burn

With mortal love to thee, and pain
That thou wouldst go, while they remain!
Life's duties first, before we try
The freedom of the moonlit sky!

GOING TO SCHOOL.

GOOD-BYE, then, Willie ! He is gone
     With shining eyes of April blue ;
     The little ones look wondering on—
' Why, what is brother going to do ? '
' I 'll not be long behind,' says Jim,
     Straightening his back, and looking bold ;
' I soon shall be a man like him—'
     —Dear little man of six years old !

O Willie, with your April eyes
     That brought the Spring of all my joy,
Even beneath these summer skies,
     I cannot spare my gentle boy !
I know the world must claim its part ;
     And you from bonds must journey free ;
But keep a corner of your heart
     Still sacred to your home and me !

My hopes go with you—here at home
     Amid the others' thoughtless play,
Towards your opening work they roam
     And linger with you all the day.

Good-bye!   God bless and prosper you,
  And fill me with His comfort full—
This day, I think, for lessons new
  Both you and I have gone to school!

A THANKSGIVING.

WITHIN the house of prayer I stand
    In praise uplifting heart and voice—
There is no mother in the land
  Has more of reason to rejoice.
For two fair sons Thou gavest me,
  And one sweet daughter, no less dear,
As David sang, I sing to Thee
  In grateful joy, devoid of fear.

For what have I to fear from Thee
  Who art my being and my end?
Within Thy presence I am free
  With the glad freedom of a friend.
There is no deed I may not dare
  Wilt Thou but sanction it, and smile;
There is no grief I cannot bear
  Wilt Thou but hold my hand the while.

These three fair children Thou hast given
  To compass me with holy mirth,
I hold in trust for Thee and heaven,
  So little is the hope of earth.
And, be 't before Thy face to stand,
  Or in the world to walk alone,
If Thou shouldst take them from my hand,
  I leave them safer in Thine own.

Father in heaven, to Thee I owe
  My life, my love, the thoughts I tell,
The dreams that with prophetic glow,
  Untold, illume my heart as well.
Thy wisdom is my spirit's air,
  Thy love the light of all my days,
Others may come to Thee with prayer,
  But I can only utter praise !

NOT mine to soar on eagle-wings
  And view the world from east to west,
To track the moorland's hidden springs,
  Or pierce the sea's mysterious breast.
  For me to sit at home is best
With common thoughts on common things—
  A cushat, brooding o'er her nest,
Her tribute to the summer brings.

Nor is the cushat's crooning call
  Unwelcome in the summer wood ;
It tells amid the pinetrees tall
  That silence is not solitude.
  It murmurs of the joys that brood
Within the sheltering forest-wall ;
  It breathes the bliss of motherhood,
And thousands mute have felt it all !

www.ingramcontent.com/pod-product-compliance
Lightning Source LLC
Chambersburg PA
CBHW022141020726
47496CB00008B/2505